# dick bruna

# miffy

D1080114

# at

# school

**EGMONT**

It's early in the morning, but

Miffy's already gone

walking to school with all her friends

and with her red dress on.

The school was not too far away

they got there very soon

the school looked very cosy and

they had a pretty room.

The teacher got up early too

she stood there at the door

and Miffy was so pleased to see

the pendant that she wore.

The bell was rung to start the day

and school could then begin

when they sat down the teacher saw

that everyone was in.

First we will make a row of curls

said teacher, do your best,

these curls will help you start to write

before you learn the rest.

Then it was time for adding up

and so the teacher drew

two toadstools and another three

Miff did the sum, can you?

They sang a very lovely song

that was their favourite thing

and teacher showed them with her hand

how fast they had to sing.

Then teacher let them build a town

with all the building blocks

with houses, churches and an arch –

there, see how grand it looks.

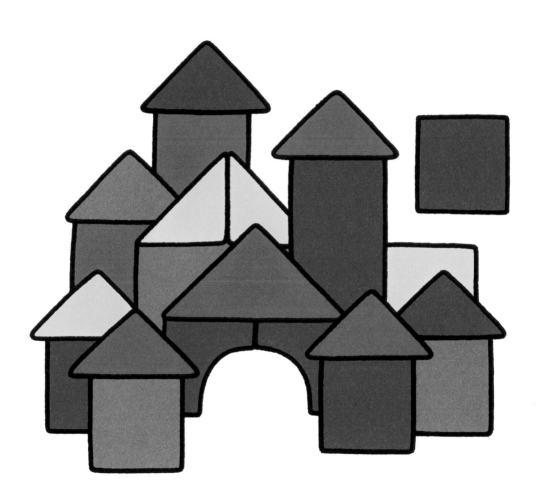

And after that they all ran out

the time for playtime came

and then they danced a little dance

and played a jolly game.

Let's do some drawing, teacher said

and Miff thought that was fine

so first she drew a bright blue sun

a tree, and then a line.

The teacher put the drawings up

they were a splendid sight

a castle, sailing boats, a house

three trees, a plane in flight ...

Now everyone sit on the ground

and I will read to you,

said teacher, and they cried, hurrah!

that was exciting, too.

Just as she finished came the bell

they all went home again

the teacher waved to them and called,

see you tomorrow, then!

# miffy's library

miffy

miffy's dream

miffy goes to stay

miffy is crying

miffy at the seaside

miffy at school

miffy at the playground

miffy at the zoo

miffy in hospital

miffy in the tent

miffy's bicycle

miffy in the snow

miffy's house

miffy at the gallery

miffy's birthday

miffy goes flying

miffy the fairy

"nijntje op school"
First published in Great Britain 1997 by Egmont Books Limited
239 Kensington High Street, London W8 6SA
Publication licensed by Mercis Publishing bv, Amsterdam
Original text Dick Bruna © copyright Mercis Publishing bv, 1984
Illustrations Dick Bruna © copyright Mercis bv, 1984
Original English translation © copyright Patricia Crampton, 1995
The moral right of the author has been asserted.
Printed in Germany by sachsendruck GmbH, Plauen
All rights reserved
ISBN 1 4052 1221 7
10 9 8 7 6 5 4 3 2 1